7 little birds in Hawaii

By Erik Jensen

Erik Jensen
7 Little Birds in Hawaii

Published by BooxAi
ISBN: 978-965-578-843-3

7 little birds in Hawaii

By Erik Jensen

7 little birds in Hawaii

By Erik Jensen

Once upon a time, on a beautiful beach in Hawaii, there perched seven little birds atop a sturdy palm tree branch. Each bird boasted feathers adorned with the vibrant colors of the tropics, their plumage a reflection of the paradise surrounding them. With the gentle sound of waves crashing against the shore, they gathered every morning, greeting the sunrise with cheerful melodies that added to the harmony of the island.

One fine morning, as the sun painted the sky in hues of orange and pink, the birds noiced a curious addition. A small nest, intricately woven with beach grasses and adorned with shells, rested in the embrace of the branch. Intrigued, they inspected the nest, wondering who the new visitors might be.

Days turned into weeks, and the seven birds witnessed a devoted mother bird diligently caring for newly hatched chicks in the nest. The little ones chirped eagerly, their tiny beaks opening wide in anticipation of their mother's return with ocean treasures.

The seven birds on the branch became enchanted by the newcomers, sharing stories of the ocean and the secrets of the sky with the growing chicks. They taught them the songs of the waves and the whispers of the trade winds, nurturing a bond that transcended generations.

As time flowed like the tides, the chicks grew stronger, their feathers reflecting the vibrant hues of the seven birds and the stunning hues of Hawaiian landscape. Together, they harmonized their melodies, blending old tunes with the rhythm of the isleand, creating a chorus that danced along the shoreline, captivating all who listened.

Seasons changed, waves rolled in and out, and the air carried the scent of plumeria. The young chicks spread their wings, taking flight for the first time, guided by the wisdom bestowed upon them by their mentors. The seven birds on the beach watched proudly as the fledglings soared above the palm trees, carrying the legacy of their shared melodies.

The beach echoed with the symphony of their songs, a testament to the bond between the seven birds and the new generation. Amidst the swaying plams and the lapping waves, their harmonious tunes continued, weaving stories of unity, love, and the eternal beauty of Hawaii.

The End

By Erik Jensen

www.ingramcontent.com/pod-product-compliance
Lightning Source LLC
Chambersburg PA
CBHW040905110726
48005CB00001B/205